The POKY LITTLE PUPPY'S
Wonderful Winter Day

By Jean Chandler • Illustrated by Sue DiCicco

A GOLDEN BOOK • NEW YORK

Copyright © 1982, 2017 by Penguin Random House LLC. All rights reserved. Published in the United States by Golden Books, an imprint of Random House Children's Books, a division of Penguin Random House LLC, 1745 Broadway, New York, NY 10019, and in Canada by Penguin Random House Canada Limited, Toronto. Originally published in the United States with different illustrations by Western Publishing Company, Inc., New York, in 1982. Golden Books, A Golden Book, A Little Golden Book, the G colophon, and the distinctive gold spine are registered trademarks of Penguin Random House LLC.
The Poky Little Puppy is a registered trademark of Penguin Random House LLC.
randomhousekids.com
Educators and librarians, for a variety of teaching tools, visit us at
RHTeachersLibrarians.com
Library of Congress Control Number: 2015952507
ISBN 978-0-399-55292-2 (trade) – ISBN 978-0-399-55360-8 (ebook)
Printed in the United States of America
10 9 8 7 6 5 4

Four frisky little puppies woke up early on a cold winter morning.

One poky little puppy was still fast asleep under his blanket.

The four frisky puppies ran to wake Mother.
"May we go out to play?" they asked.

"Yes," said Mother, "after you eat your oatmeal."

Then the poky little puppy woke up.
  "I smell oatmeal with milk and honey!"
he said.

He got to his bowl just in time to see his brothers and sisters racing out the door.

"Hurry, Poky," they called. "We're all going out to play!"

The poky little puppy finished his breakfast and ran outside. His brothers and sisters were nowhere in sight.

But there was a surprise. Snowflakes were falling everywhere.

The poky little puppy heard children laughing. He heard a shovel scraping on the walk. And he felt the snowflakes falling gently on his nose, his ears, and his curly little tail.

There were paw prints in the snow.
The poky little puppy followed the
paw prints around the bird bath . . .

. . . and past the woodpile.
He bumped right into his brother!

Another little puppy was peeking out from
behind a tree.

Two more puppies came burrowing through a snowdrift.

Four little puppies ran and romped
and rolled in the snow. The snow was
soft and wet and cold.

It was also slippery! The puppies went slipping and sliding down a little hill— one, two, three, four.

But where was the poky little puppy?

He was having a ride on a sled with a friend.

The puppies dug tunnels in the snow—
one, two, three, four.

But where was that poky little puppy now?

He was making a snow angel with a friend.
His angel looked like a fat little sausage!

One little puppy stopped playing. "I smell something good," he said.

"It's dinner!" said the others. So home they went as fast as they could go—one, two, three, four.

But where was that poky little puppy *now*?

He was chasing snowballs with his friends.
That was the most fun of all!

When the poky little puppy finally got home,
his brothers and sisters had finished eating.
His dinner was almost cold.

And he was so tired that he fell asleep
before he could finish his favorite dessert—
strawberry shortcake.

Mother tucked them all in—one, two, three, four, five little puppies, all happily dreaming of their wonderful winter day.